Living with Vampires

by

Jeremy Strong

Illustrated by Scoular Anderson

You do not need to read this page – just get on with the book!

First published in 2000 in Great Britain by
Barrington Stoke Ltd, Sandeman House, Trunk's Close,
55 High Street, Edinburgh EH1 1SR

Reprinted 2001, 2002, 2003, 2004, 2005

ISBN 1-902260-67-8

Printed in Great Britain by Bell & Bain Ltd

Meet The Author - Jeremy Strong

What is your favourite animal?

A cat

What is your favourite boy's name?

Magnus Pinchbottom

What is your favourite girl's name?

Wobbly Wendy

What is your favourite food?

Chicken Kiev (I love garlic)

What is your favourite music?

Soft

What is your favourite hobby?

Sleeping

Meet The Illustrator - Scoular Anderson

What is your favourite animal?

Humorous dogs

What is your favourite boy's name?

Orlando

What is your favourite girl's name?

Esmerelda

What is your favourite food?

Garlicky, tomatoey pasta

What is your favourite music?

Big orchestras

What is your favourite hobby?

Long walks

Contents

Chapter 1
No Escape!

Kevin Vladd was not looking forward to Tuesday evening.

His parents, Mr and Mrs Vladd, were not looking forward to Tuesday evening.

And his teacher, Mrs Fottle, was not looking forward to Tuesday evening either.

Tuesday was the date set for Parent-Teacher Meetings at Molehill Junior School.

Almost four hundred parents would meet up with eight teachers. There would be face-to-face encounters of a dangerous kind. There was no escape.

Kevin Vladd always felt nervous about these meetings. He usually got on quite well with his teacher, Mrs Fottle. But he was never sure what she was going to say to his parents.

He did *try* to work at school. It was just that sometimes he had better things to do. He could sit and stare out of the window for hours, watching things. Look at that cloud! It was shaped like an elephant! An elephant with a space shuttle sticking out of its head.

And if there weren't any clouds to gaze at, he could always feast his eyes on Miranda Nightingale. Miranda had long,

black hair. Miranda had the face of a princess. Miranda had dark and liquid eyes, like secret pools.

Kevin thought that Miranda Nightingale was Heaven on Legs.

The problem was that every other boy in the school thought so too and Grant Doobey even more than most.

However, now that Tuesday evening had arrived, Kevin had other things on his mind. Kevin and his parents were waiting for Mrs Fottle to finish talking to Mrs Doobey and Grant. Kevin could hear their low voices mumbling away on the other side of the classroom door. Kevin began to wonder what Mrs Fottle would say about him. He hoped it would be something nice.

Kevin quite liked Mrs Fottle. She was one of those quiet, middle-aged teachers.

CHRISTMAS
DISCO

She had a middle-sized, shapeless body that she kept in a shapeless cardigan. Even Mrs Fottle's car was a bit shapeless. Most of the time she was kind and helpful and said nice things. Most of the time.

His parents had not met Mrs Fottle before, but he was nervous. He hoped that everything would go well. He knew his parents had not eaten before they came out. Kevin did not dare think about what they might do if they were hungry. It was too late to do anything about it now.

The classroom door opened and Mrs Doobey came out, pushing Grant in front of her. Grant and Kevin glanced at each other. They were not good friends. In fact, they were bad enemies. Grant stuck out his tongue and then pretended to cut his throat with one finger. Kevin looked away. He followed his parents into the classroom.

Kevin Vladd

Mrs Fottle gave Mr and Mrs Vladd a rather weak smile. "Kevin's maths has improved," she began, "but I have to say that I am rather worried about him."

Kevin sat bolt upright. What *had* he done? Had Mrs Fottle spotted him flicking paper pellets at the back of Grant Doobey's head? Or even worse, had she seen him staring at Miranda Nightingale?

Mr Vladd leaned forward a little. He was watching Mrs Fottle closely. Rather too closely, Kevin thought.

"What's the problem?" he asked.

Mrs Fottle opened a folder of work and pulled out a picture. "I asked everyone to draw a picture of their father or mother," said Mrs Fottle. "I am afraid that Kevin drew this. There's an awful lot of blood in it, don't you think?"

She held up the picture and Kevin's parents studied it. He had drawn his father. He had drawn him with Dracula fangs. Blood was dripping from them.

Mrs Vladd clapped her hands with delight and beamed at her husband. "Darling, it looks just like you!"

Mrs Fottle was not amused. She began to huff and puff. "Mrs Vladd, this is no joke. I am beginning to wonder if you let your son watch too many horror films. This kind of drawing is *very* disturbing. And it's not the first time he's handed in a picture like this either."

Mrs Fottle pulled out several more examples. "Look at this one – zombies! And this one – vampires! I really think Kevin ought to see a social worker. All that blood. He has such a violent imagination."

Mr Vladd smiled. "The thing is, Mrs Fottle, it's not in his imagination." Mr Vladd lifted back his upper lip and showed her his teeth.

Mrs Fottle took one look at Mr Vladd's milk-white, needle-sharp fangs and turned very pale. "Oh," she whispered. "Oh, dear." Her eyes went big and round. "I think I'm going to faint." And she did. She slumped forwards across her desk.

Mrs Vladd clapped her hands again. "Supper!" she cried, looking at Mrs Fottle in glee. "I'm starving." Kevin's parents sank their teeth into Mrs Fottle's neck.

Kevin's parents were Grade Three vampires. No wonder he was worried.

GRADE ONE
GRADE TWO
GRADE THREE
STOP
GRADE FOUR

Chapter 2
All You Need To Know About Vampires

There are four kinds of vampires.

Grade One are the most dangerous. They only appear at night. They spend the daytime lying in their coffins. These are the ones you often see in films or read about in books. They have the fangs, the dripping blood and the white faces. They can turn into bats and fly about. They suck blood and leave lots of bodies around, which is rather thoughtless and very untidy.

Grade Two vampires are not so powerful. They can also turn into bats. They leave lots of dead bodies around too, which is not very nice if you happen to step on one. Like the Grade Ones, Grade Two vamps only come out at night, but they don't have coffins. During the day, they just lie about in damp, dark caves, getting wet and muddy.

Grade Three vampires can wander about during daylight. They suck people's blood, but they can't kill anyone. Their victims usually faint and when they wake up they can't remember what happened to them. This is just as well. The worst thing that Grade Three vampires can do is turn people into zombies, but even that wears off after a while. They don't hang about in coffins or caves. They live in ordinary homes and sleep in ordinary beds, which is very sensible of them.

Grade Four vampires are totally hopeless. They can't even suck blood. They just sort of lick your skin, which is pretty revolting. All the other vampires reckon that Grade Fours are Totally Pathetic And A Big Joke.

However, if *your* parents are vampires, it's no joke at all. Even if they're only Grade Three.

Kevin Vladd was unlucky in another way. He was the only non-vampire in his family. There is an old saying that every one hundred years each vampire family produces *one* child who is *not* a vampire. Kevin was that child.

What Kevin wanted more than anything else was to have normal parents. He wanted to be able to go outside with them without wondering if they were going to sink their fangs into some poor, unsuspecting member of the public.

Most of all he wanted to go to the Christmas Disco. He wanted to dance with Miranda Nightingale, the most beautiful girl in the school – if not the world, or even the universe.

The problem was that the disco was for staff, children and their parents. If Kevin went to the Christmas Disco, his parents would have to go too.

Mr and Mrs Vladd liked discos. But Kevin hadn't even told them about it yet. How could he take a pair of vampires to a disco? Anything could happen.

Kevin gave a heavy sigh. Mr and Mrs Vladd had just finished feeding on poor Mrs

Fottle. Now they were delicately wiping the blood from their fangs with some paper tissues.

Mrs Vladd smiled at her son. "Stop looking so worried, Kevin. Mrs Fottle said that your maths has improved."

"Mum, I'm not worried about maths," Kevin pointed out. "What about Mrs Fottle?"

"Oh, she'll be all right, you know she will. When she wakes up she won't remember a thing. Now, what's all this about a Christmas Disco?"

Mrs Vladd pointed at the big poster on the classroom wall. "You haven't said a thing about it. I thought you liked discos." She grabbed his arm playfully. "Are we all going?"

Kevin let out another sigh. When he was with his parents he spent a lot of his time sighing.

Chapter 3
How To Cure A Vampire

After the Parent-Teacher meeting, Mrs Fottle had to take three days off work. She said she felt drained. She couldn't remember what had happened, which was a small blessing. But it was all too much for Kevin.

He decided that things couldn't go on like this. It was so shaming. And it was dangerous.

The Christmas Disco was coming up. He was desperate to go. But if he went, his parents would go too. Miranda Nightingale would be there. How could he put her in such danger?

Kevin knew that somehow he would have to cure his parents of being vampires and he had five days to find out how to do it.

He sat in his bedroom and thought and thought. And then it came to him.

Garlic!

Vampires can't stand garlic. Everyone knows that. Maybe, if he could get his parents to eat a lot of garlic, it would put them off being vampires.

Kevin searched the cookery books in the kitchen. It took a little while, but in the end he found the ideal dish. It was called

Chicken Kiev. Chicken breast stuffed with garlic butter.

Mum was surprised when Kevin told her he wanted to cook a meal for everyone.

"You can't even make toast without burning it," she said.

"This is going to be a really big surprise," Kevin promised.

"All right. What are you going to make?"

"Aha! You are not allowed into the kitchen."

Kevin got to work. The recipe said that he should use two cloves of garlic. Kevin wanted the meal to cure his parents of being vampires for the rest of their lives, so he put in thirty cloves altogether. He was thrilled. He was sure this was going to

work. His parents would never want to bite another neck.

The smell in the kitchen was wonderful. Kevin boiled some potatoes and some peas to go with the chicken. He laid the table and called for his parents.

"It does smell nice," said Dad.

"What is it?"

"Try it and see," said Kevin.

Mr and Mrs Vladd stuffed the chicken into their mouths. Dad began to cough. He spluttered. He choked. He fell backwards off his chair. His legs kicked up under the table and his plateful of Chicken Kiev was catapulted through the air. It went zooming across the room like some weird alien UFO and smashed through the window.

At the same time Mrs Vladd went mad. Her eyes were as big as plates. Her tongue was hanging out of her mouth and flapping about like a pink flag in a storm. She leaped from her chair and began to dance. She hopped from one foot to the other, flapping her arms wildly, as if she wanted to take off.

Suddenly she rushed to the bathroom and threw herself beneath the shower. She

didn't seem to care that she still had all her clothes on. She stood there with her mouth open, gulping down cold water.

Meanwhile Mr Vladd was lying on the floor outside the bathroom. He was groaning and frothing at the mouth. Kevin grabbed a jug full of water and poured it down Dad's throat.

The Vladds spent the next day in bed. Kevin was banned from cooking anything for the rest of his life.

Kevin didn't mind about being banned from the kitchen. What worried him was that he still had the same problem. How could he cure his parents of being vampires in time for the Christmas Disco?

And if he didn't go to the Christmas Disco he knew who would dance with Miranda Nightingale. Grant Doobey of course.

Chapter 4
Big Feet, Big Trouble

Grant Doobey was the tallest boy in the school. He was the most handsome boy in the school. He was also the most big-headed boy on the planet and a bit of a bully.

Kevin hated Grant.

Grant hated Kevin.

Hate at first sight.

Out in the playground Kevin kept well out of Grant's way, because Grant had long arms, with fists on the end of them. He also had long legs, with boots.

For some strange reason, Miranda Nightingale seemed to like Grant Doobey. Kevin couldn't understand why. It made him despair. What kind of chance did he have?

Even more worrying was the fact that he hadn't managed to cure his parents yet.

Kevin decided to go to the School Library and see what he could find out about vampires. Maybe he could pick up some useful information.

Sadly, there was only one book about vampires and it was written like a cheap comic. It was full of useless jokes.

"Ha ha," muttered Kevin. "I shan't tell my parents that one. They'd die laughing … I don't think."

He was just beginning to get fed up when Miranda Nightingale drifted into the library. Kevin almost fell off his chair. He looked around. He was alone with Miranda! This was his big chance. He could ask her to dance with him at the Christmas Disco!

Miranda saw Kevin and wandered across. She stood so close that Kevin could hear her breathing. She looked at him without smiling. Kevin could not remember seeing her smile, ever. He would love to make her smile. But for the moment he just stared up at her with his mouth open.

"Why are you reading a book about vampires?" she asked.

Kevin shrugged. "No reason. It was just lying here."

Miranda nodded. There was a long silence. Kevin thought, I must stop staring at her or she'll think I'm staring at her! Kevin looked at Miranda's feet instead. She was wearing a pair of dinky, pink trainers with glittery laces.

Kevin's brain had turned to jelly and was slopping about uselessly inside his head. What should he say? He must say *something*. "What size shoes do you wear?" he croaked. Even as he spoke he thought,

Kevin Vladd, you are the biggest dumbo in dumbo-land.

Miranda hit him with the vampire book. *Blipp!* "Are you saying I've got big feet? You are *so* rude!" *Blapp!* Miranda hit him again and stormed out of the library.

Kevin sat there and cursed himself. How could he have been so stupid? Why hadn't he asked her to the disco? Why did he ask her about shoe sizes?

He grabbed the vampire book and went stamping back to the bookcase. He was just shoving it back when he spotted another book lying on the shelf.

ALL ABOUT HYPNOSIS.

Chapter 5
Look Into My Eyes ...

The more Kevin read, the more excited he became. The book said that hypnosis could be used to stop people smoking, or snoring, or eating too much. You could use hypnosis to make people behave the way you wanted them to behave.

In other words, Kevin could use hypnosis to stop his parents being vampires. All he had to do was to put them in a trance.

Kevin would need something to dangle in front of his parents. They would stare at it and he would make it swing from side to side. They would slowly slip into a trance. Then he could tell them to do anything he wanted. Brilliant!

As soon as he got home that afternoon Kevin got out his yo-yo and practised in front of the mirror. He swung the yo-yo gently, backwards and forwards. He fixed his eyes on it. He spoke softly to himself.

"You are feeling sleepy ... you are feeling sleepy ..."

BANG!!

He fell asleep and crashed to the floor. It had worked! All he had to do now was to try the same trick on his parents and hypnotise them.

Mr and Mrs Vladd were in the front room, watching TV. Kevin gave them an innocent smile. "Can I show you a trick with my yo-yo?" said Kevin.

"Does it have anything to do with garlic?" Mr Vladd asked.

"Of course not!" said Kevin, pretending to look shocked.

"Will it take long?" Mrs Vladd wanted to get back to watching TV.

"No. Time will fly," Kevin promised, keeping his fingers crossed behind his back.

Kevin sat his parents next to each other and dangled the yo-yo in front of them. He began to make it swing backwards and forwards. "Watch my yo-yo very carefully," he began. He made his voice sound soft and even. The yo-yo went back and forth. Mum

and Dad's eyeballs went back and forth. Their heads began to rock gently. Mrs Vladd's tongue slopped out of her mouth.

"You are feeling sleepy," Kevin said. "Your eyelids are drooping. They are getting heavier and heavier. You can't keep your eyes open any longer. You are asleep ... asleep ... deeply asleep."

Mum began to snore. Dad leaned towards her. Soon they were propping each other up, fast asleep.

Kevin went on. "You will never want to suck blood again. You are going to stop being Grade Three vampires. You are going to be ordinary, nice people."

He stopped and looked at his parents. They were still asleep. Mr Vladd was snoring. Mrs Vladd was dribbling. Things were looking good. But Kevin wanted to be sure that the hypnosis was working. Kevin decided to carry out one or two tests.

"Raise your right arm," he said. Slowly but surely they both raised their right arms. Kevin's heart skipped a beat. It was working! His parents were in his power! He could make them do – ANYTHING!

"Dad, stick your finger in Mum's ear." Kevin began giggling.

"Mum, stick your finger up Dad's nose."

He couldn't go on. He was laughing too much. It was *not* a pretty sight.

The important thing was that he had proved the hypnosis was working. "On the count of three you will both wake up. You will not remember that you were hypnotised. One, two, three!"

It was a pity that Kevin had forgotten to tell them to remove their fingers. They took one look at what they were doing and hastily snatched away their hands. They gave each other strange looks.

"What's been going on?" asked Mr Vladd.

"I was showing you a trick with my yo-yo," Kevin said and gave them an innocent smile.

"Oh." They both nodded, puzzled. They shifted their chairs away from each other, as if they didn't trust each other.

And that was that. All Kevin could do now was sit back and wait and see. Were his parents truly cured of being vampires?

Chapter 6
The Letter

Three days passed. Kevin's parents didn't sink their teeth into any living thing. It was wonderful. He felt as if a dreadful weight had been lifted from his shoulders. He no longer had to live in the shadow of vampire parents.

He could go to the Christmas Disco in complete safety and so could everyone else. All he had to do now was see if he could get

Miranda Nightingale to dance with him. Maybe she would if he said he was sorry about asking her shoe size.

There was only one day to go, so Kevin didn't have much time. The problem was that Miranda always seemed to have a huge crowd of boys around her. They followed her round like zombies, most of all Grant Doobey. It was impossible to get a private moment with her.

Kevin decided that he would write her a letter. He worked on it all the way through the maths lesson. He had to get it just right. He sat there, staring at his work, sucking his pencil. There was a strange drone in one ear. Kevin tried to blot it out, but it went on and on.

"Kevin? Kevin? Are you with us Kevin? Is there anyone in? Kevin?"

It was Mrs Fottle. She was standing next to him, gazing down. She shook her head. "You were in a world of your own. I was going to ask if you could tell us what we call a triangle with three equal sides." Mrs Fottle raised her eyebrows. "But I can see that you are far too busy with something more important. Let's see what you've been writing. No, don't cover it up. I want to have a look. Thank you."

Mrs Fottle picked up the letter. She began to read it out loud. "*I never meant to say that you have got big feet.*"

The rest of the class began to giggle. Mrs Fottle read on and her eyebrows climbed higher and higher up her forehead. "*I think you have the most beautiful feet in the world.*"

Great splutters of laughter exploded around the class. Some kids were clutching

their sides. "*I would die to have feet like yours.*"

Now half the class were rolling about on the floor.

Mrs Fottle slowly put the note back on Kevin's desk. "Well," she began, "I wonder who this note is for? Would you like to tell us?"

Kevin wanted to die. How could he tell everyone in the class that it was for Miranda Nightingale? He was certain she was staring at him. Her eyes were burning holes in his skin. Kevin knew that if he said the letter was for her she would never, ever speak to him again.

Kevin looked up at his teacher. He swallowed hard. "It's for you, Mrs Fottle."

At least that stopped everyone laughing. They were so gobsmacked that they just sat and stared with their mouths open.

Mrs Fottle knew perfectly well it wasn't meant for her. What she did next was something that Kevin would remember for the rest of his life.

"Of course, it's private," she said. "I'm very sorry, Kevin, I should never have read it at all."

And she really meant it. The class stopped laughing. There wasn't even a snigger. Mrs Fottle went back to her desk and sat down. She began talking about triangles again.

But Kevin couldn't write his letter after that. The damage had been done. He would never be able to speak to Miranda now. His whole life was a mess.

As soon as he got home Kevin went upstairs and threw himself on his bed. He had managed to stop his parents being vampires, but the one thing he really wanted he would never get now.

It was only when Kevin opened up his school bag that he discovered the note. It was tucked down between his books. He unfolded it carefully.

Dear Kevin,

Those were such sweet things to say about my feet. I would like to dance with you at the disco. See you there!

Love, Miranda xxx

Kevin read the letter at least fifty times.

Chapter 7
The Christmas Disco

The moment Kevin walked into the school hall on disco night, he knew he would remember it forever. Mr and Mrs Vladd hadn't done anything vampirish for over a week now. Kevin was sure that the hypnosis had worked. Their blood-sucking days were over.

The hall looked fabulous. There were glittery decorations dangling from the ceiling. Coloured lights were flashing round the walls and bouncing off a twirling glitter ball. Everything seemed to sparkle and Kevin's heart was already dancing.

The disco was in full swing. Music was pounding. It was so loud it seemed to be jumping out of the hall walls. Kevin searched around in the darkness for Miranda.

"Come and dance!" He heard a voice behind him.

Kevin swung round. It was Mum. She seized him and began to twirl around. Kevin forced a smile, but he could have died with shame. He prayed that Miranda wouldn't see him dancing with his own mother.

All at once he saw Miranda for a moment. She was sitting on the far side of the hall. Her dress sparkled. Her hair sparkled. She looked like an angel, but an angel with a frown. Once again Kevin longed to make her smile.

There were boys all around her, but she wasn't dancing. Grant Doobey was standing beside her, saying something, but she wasn't even looking at him.

Kevin smiled and felt for the letter that he had carefully put in his pocket. He knew Miranda was waiting just for him. In a moment he would be dancing with her. He began to make his way across the hall.

"Kevin! Come and dance. Tell me you've forgiven me." This time it was Mrs Fottle.

This disco was becoming a nightmare! First of all his mother and now his teacher!

"I can't," began Kevin, but Mrs Fottle clutched him to her chest and whirled him round until he was dizzy.

"You're a wonderful dancer," she said, but his feet had hardly touched the ground.

"I've got to go now," Kevin said, tearing himself away. "Thank you for the dance."

He hurried off. Where was Miranda? Her chair was empty. The crowd of boys had gone too. Kevin's heart began to beat faster. He mustn't lose her now! He pushed his way through the dancers.

And that was when the screaming began.

People began to rush past, wild-eyed with terror. Squealing girls scattered in all directions. Boys rushed about like headless chickens. Parents and teachers clutched at each other for safety.

But why?

And then Kevin saw the first zombie. It was Grant Doobey. He was striding through the hall, his arms stretched out in front of him. His face was white and his eyes had rolled up inside his skull. He looked revolting.

Kevin glanced at Grant's neck. Yes! He could see two fang-holes. Kevin's heart sank into his boots. The hypnosis had worn off. His parents had gone back to their vampire ways.

Behind Grant was another zombie and another and another! Now there were zombies everywhere. They were stomping through the crowded disco and all around them people screamed and waved their

arms helplessly and fainted in great big heaps.

Behind the zombies Kevin could see his parents. They hadn't had any fresh blood for two weeks and now they had a whole larder full of humans around them. This was the disaster he had been trying to prevent all along.

Kevin's heart suddenly lurched back out of his boots. Miranda! She was in danger! She was standing right next to his parents, watching the mayhem. She was still frowning. She seemed unaware of the peril she was in. He must save her!

Kevin dashed across the hall, crashing through the screaming dancers. He pushed the zombies aside. He hurled himself past his parents and grabbed Miranda.

"This way!" he shouted. "I'll save you! I'll get you out of here! Come on!" Together, Kevin and Miranda ran to the hall door. "Don't let go of my hand! Come on, this way. We'll be safe down here!"

They raced down the dark corridor. Kevin threw open the library door and hid amongst the bookcases, panting madly.

At last they got their breath back. Kevin could feel Miranda standing right next to him. He could almost hear her heart beating.

She was still gripping his hand.

Kevin wanted this moment to last forever. Alone at last with Miranda Nightingale. She gazed at him.

"You are so brave, Kevin," she said. He turned and looked at her and at last she smiled at him.

Even in that darkness it was a truly dazzling smile.

And that was when Kevin realised that it was not his parents who had caused the mayhem after all.

Miranda Nightingale had fangs. *She* was the vampire.

And he had left his yo-yo at home.

Who is Barrington Stoke?

Barrington Stoke was a famous and much-loved story-teller. He travelled from village to village carrying a lantern to light his way. He arrived as it grew dark and when the young boys and girls of the village saw the glow of his lantern, they hurried to the central meeting place. They were full of excitement and expectation, for his stories were always wonderful.

Then Barrington Stoke set down his lantern. In the flickering light the listeners were enthralled by his tales of adventure, horror and mystery. He knew exactly what they liked best and he loved telling a good story. And another. And then another. When the lantern burned low and dawn was nearly breaking, he slipped away. He was gone by morning, only to appear the next day in some other village to tell the next story.

Barrington Stoke would like to thank all its readers for commenting on the manuscript before publication and in particular:

Lewis Ball
Stewart Dennis
Jack Fookes
Sandra Hart
Tom Gaughtrie
Andrew Johnston
Fiona Morecroft
Maeve Mowbray
Tahmeen Rahman
Hannah Smith
Charlie Suen
Loretta Suen

If you loved this story, why don't you read ...

Problems with a Python

by Jeremy Strong

Have you ever looked after a friend's pet? Adam agrees to look after Gary's python, but things get wildly out of hand when he decides to take her to school to impress his friends.